FARGO PUB

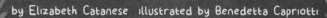

by Elizabeth Catanese   illustrated by Benedetta Capriotti

MT. OLYMPUS THEME PARK
THE SPIDER
DRAMA

Spellbound

An Imprint of Magic Wagon
abdobooks.com

To Dylan Joseph Catanese and Escher Paul Catanese,
with love. –EC

To Cristina, Nino, Benedetta and Giuseppe. –BC

abdobooks.com

Published by Magic Wagon, a division of ABDO, PO Box 398166,
Minneapolis, Minnesota 55439. Copyright © 2022 by Abdo Consulting
Group, Inc. International copyrights reserved in all countries. No
part of this book may be reproduced in any form without written
permission from the publisher. Spellbound™ is a trademark and logo
of Magic Wagon.

Printed in the United States of America, North Mankato, Minnesota.
052021
092021

 THIS BOOK CONTAINS
RECYCLED MATERIALS

Written by Elizabeth Catanese
Illustrated by Benedetta Capriotti
Edited by Bridget O'Brien
Art Directed by Laura Graphenteen

Library of Congress Control Number: 2020947949

Publisher's Cataloging-in-Publication Data

Names: Catanese, Elizabeth, author. | Capriotti, Benedetta, illustrator.
Title: The spider drama / by Elizabeth Catanese ; illustrated by Benedetta Capriotti.
Description: Minneapolis, Minnesota : Magic Wagon, 2022. | Series: Mt. Olympus theme park
Summary: After receiving a text from her perfect twin sister Cassie claiming she's in trouble
    at their theater club's trip to Mt. Olympus Theme Park, Anna goes to help her, but finds
    herself in the middle of a myth involving Athena, knitting, and Cassie, who's been turned
    into a spider.
Identifiers: ISBN 9781098230418 (lib. bdg.) | ISBN 9781098230975 (ebook) | ISBN 9781098231255
    (Read-to-Me ebook)
Subjects: LCSH: Amusement parks--Juvenile fiction. | Mythology, Greek--Juvenile
    fiction. | Siblings--Juvenile fiction. | Knitting--Juvenile fiction. | Spiders--Juvenile fiction.
    | Amusement rides--Juvenile fiction. | Gods, Greek--Juvenile fiction
Classification: DDC [FIC]--dc23

Table of Contents

ATHENA'S WORLD

Chapter 1
A SURPRISE

Anna sees the cast list **posted** outside Mr. Morpheus's theater club classroom. But her twin sister *runs* there first.

Cassie is older by one minute. She is usually one minute FASTER, too. ANNOYING!

"**WOOT**!" Cassie high-fives

her friends. "I'm Athena!"

Anna **slumps** into her desk.

She is Chorus Member #3.

Anna *wrote* the play, *Athena and Arachne*, for theater club. It is based on an ancient Greek story called a **myth**. But Mr. Morpheus gave her sister the lead role. **RUDE**!

"Now that you have all seen your roles, I have a surprise," says Mr. Morpheus.

"Tomorrow you don't have to go to class. We're going to learn more about our characters by going to Mt. Olympus Theme Park for the WHOLE day!"

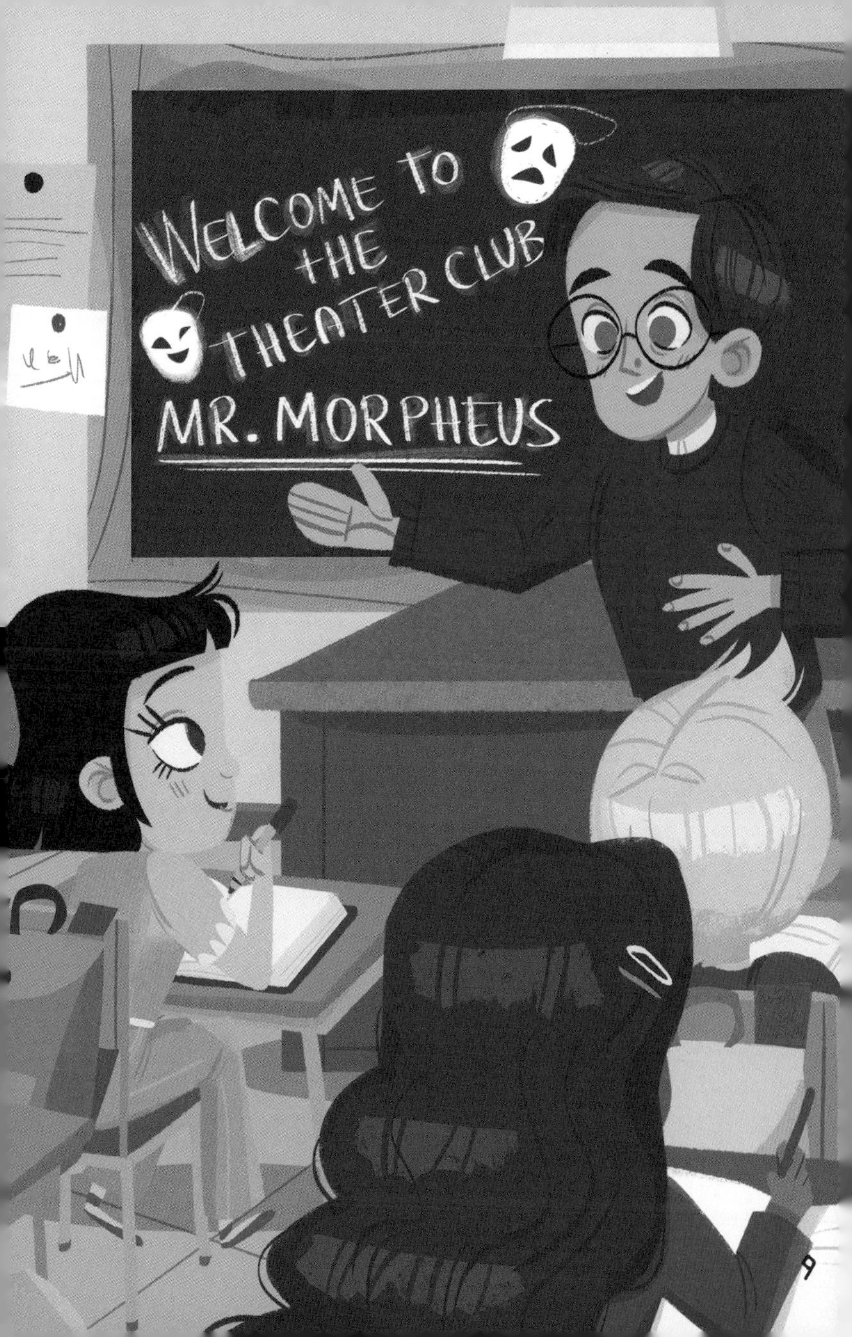
WELCOME TO
THE
THEATER CLUB
MR. MORPHEUS

Half the class cheers or **groans**. Mt. Olympus Theme Park, an amusement park based on Greek **myths**, is a love it or leave it place.

Anna usually **loves** it. But not when Cassie gets the lead role in a play Anna wrote!

"You're a better *writer*, but I'm a better actor," says Cassie on their walk home.

In Anna's play, the goddess Athena turns her friend Arachne into a *spider* after she loses to her in a contest. Anna sometimes gets *jealous* of Cassie. She wishes she could turn her into a spider, too.

But Cassie is right. Last year, when they performed *Merry Shoppins*, Anna forgot one of her lines. It was the last line of the play. Awkward.

"I'm taking a mental **HEALTH**
day tomorrow," says Anna.

Anna and Cassie LIVE with their grandma. Grandma lets them take three mental health days per year. They can stay home from school even if they're not SICK.

"Stop being a **baby**," says Cassie.

Anna *sighs*. She hates it when Cassie plays the "older sister" card. Besides, Anna has **BiG** plans for her day. She is going to make a PURPLE scarf for Grandma's birthday present.

Chapter II

GRAPE JELLY SANDWICH

Anna is working on her scarf when her phone **buzzes**. It's a text from Cassie. "Help! I'm trapped in Athena's web. Come ASAP."

"Nice try," Anna *writes*. "No."

"GRAPE JELLY SANDWICH,"
Cassie texts. That is the CODE the
twins use when one is in trouble.
It's only for real EMERGENCIES.

Anna **SHOVES** her scarf and
knitting needles into her backpack.
She grabs two tokens to take the
bus to Mt. Olympus Theme Park.

As she *knits* on the ride over,
she looks at Cassie's text again.
Athena's *web*? She doesn't
remember that ride.

Mr. Morpheus **SPOTS** Anna walking through the gates of Mt. Olympus Theme Park.

"We can't find Cassie! Have you **heard** from her? We were all in Athena's World, on the NEW Athena's Web Net Climber. It's 40 feet of webbing that you climb.

"Cassie made it to the top first. Then she was **gone**. I asked the attendant to take me to the other side. But there's **NOTHING**. Cassie just disappeared."

"I'll **find** her," says Anna.

Mr. Morpheus PULLS Anna through the crowd to the front of the line. It looks like a long way up.

Anna wipes the **SWEAT** off her forehead when she gets to the top. Mr. Morpheus is right. There is nothing at the top.

BAM! A giant spider knocks Anna off the web. She falls forward, down, down, down and **THWAK** onto the dirt.

Chapter III

AN UNFRIENDLY COMPETITION

"You must be Anna," says the **spider**. "My name is Darla. I'm Arachne's twin sister. I need your HELP."

For a minute, Anna thinks she is imagining Darla, the **GIANT** spider. But the spider speaks again. Anna is not at Mt. Olympus anymore! She is in a real Greek myth.

"Arachne is in a knitting contest with your sister and the goddess, Athena. Athena turned me into a spider two weeks ago for drinking her ORANGE soda by mistake.

"Our sisters got turned into **spiders** today too! Athena says she'll turn the WINNER of the contest back into a person."

Darla brings Anna to where a woman wearing a white dress is knitting a purple scarf. Two spiders are also knitting purple scarves. They are STUCK in a big web.

"I'm Athena," says the woman in white. "You must be here to JUDGE our knitting competition!"

"Ummm... I don't think I am here to—"

"I ate a **delicious** grape jelly sandwich today," spider Cassie shouts from the web.

Anna understands Cassie's **SIGNAL**. "Yes, I'm the judge."

When they're done, Anna looks at the scarves. Cassie's is a beautiful **star** stitch. No mistakes. Perfect fringe. Arachne's has silk woven in. It **SHINES** in the light.

Athena used at least twenty different shades of purple yarn. Each scarf is great. But Anna knows something important from *writing* her play.

"The WINNER is Athena,"

says Anna. Cassie gasps.

"You're all in luck," says Athena.

"I'm going to turn everyone back

into a person. Then we will have a

party to **CELEBRATE** my win!"

"Let's get out of here!" Anna says. She **GRABS** Cassie's hand. The back of the Net Climber from Mt. Olympus **APPEARS**. Anna and Cassie begin to climb.

Chapter IV

REWRITING THE SCRIPT

PLOP. Anna and Cassie plop down on the pavement at Mt. Olympus Theme Park. Mr. Morpheus and the theater club are **gathered** around them.

"Are you OK?"
Mr. Morpheus asks.

41

"We're GREAT," says Cassie. "I got turned into a spider by Athena, but Anna saved me."

"Thank goodness you're OK," says Mr. Morpheus.

"Anna **DESERVES** the part of Athena," Cassie continues. "She totally knows Athena better than me. Anna knew that Athena had to win the knitting contest to be happy enough to turn me back into a person."

"Then Anna can play the part of Athena!" **EXCLAIMS** Mr. Morpheus.

"I have a better idea," says Anna. "I'd like to *write* a new part for the play. I think Arachne should have a twin sister named Darla."

Mr. Morpheus laughs. "You are so **creative**, Anna."

On the bus back to school, Anna and Cassie join their purple scarf projects into one. "Grandma's gonna love this," Cassie says. "We're a GREAT team," Anna replies.